Fox Tails

The Biggest Roller Coaster

Tina Kügler

ACORN™
SCHOLASTIC INC.

For my grandma, who rode the Demon
at Great America, because I was
too scared to do it.–TK

Library of Congress Cataloging-in-Publication Data

Names: Kügler, Tina, author, illustrator. Title: The biggest roller coaster / by Tina Kügler. Description: First edition. | New York : Acorn/Scholastic, 2020. | Series: Fox tails ; 2 | Summary: Fox siblings Fritz and Franny, and their patient dog Fred, are at the amusement park squabbling about which ride is fastest and loudest—but when they are confronted by the biggest, tallest, and loudest roller coaster they decide that maybe Fred would prefer something not quite so scary. Identifiers: LCCN 2019041179 ISBN 9781338561692 (paperback) | ISBN 9781338561708 (library binding) | ISBN 9781338635157 (ebk) Subjects: LCSH: Roller coasters—Juvenile fiction. | Amusement parks—Juvenile fiction. | Brothers and sisters—Juvenile fiction. | Choice (Psychology)—Juvenile fiction. | Dogs—Juvenile fiction. | CYAC: Roller coasters—Fiction. | Amusement parks—Fiction. | Brothers and sisters—Fiction. | Choice—Fiction. | Foxes—Fiction. | Dogs—Fiction. Classification: LCC PZ7.1.K844 Bi 2020 | DDC [E]—dc23 LC record available at https://lccn.loc.gov/2019041179

10 9 8 7 6 5 4 3 2 1   20 21 22 23 24

Printed in China   62

First edition, November 2020

Edited by Katie Carella

Book design by Sarah Dvojack

Let's Go

This is Fritz.

This is Franny.

This is Fred.

4

9

This ride is fast.

THIS ride is loud and fast!

17

Tallest, Fastest, Loudest

23

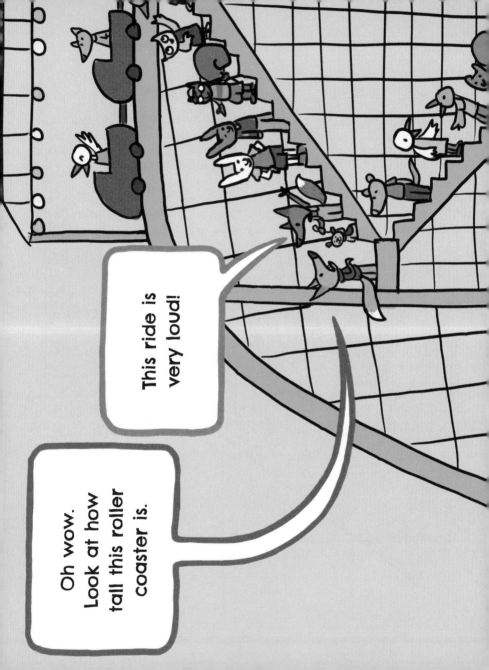

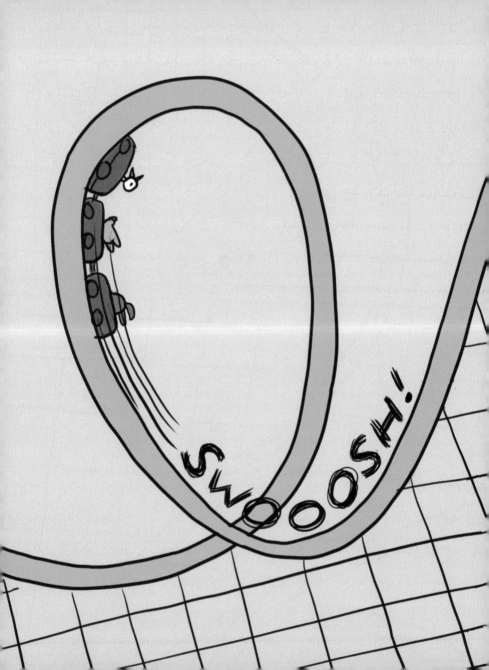

I think this ride is too loud for Fred.

The Perfect Ride

Look, Fred.
There are so many rides.

Too fast.

40

41

About the Author

Tina Kügler lives in Los Angeles with her husband and three sons. She was afraid of roller coasters when she was younger, but now she likes them. Her favorites are: The Beast at Kings Island  in Ohio, GhostRider at Knott's Berry Farm in California, and Expedition Everest at Animal Kingdom in Florida.

Tina writes and illustrates books, and also draws cartoons for television. She wrote and illustrated the SNAIL AND WORM beginning reader series and was awarded a Theodor Seuss Geisel Honor in 2018.

Oh, and she also has a cranky lizard named Jabba, a shy cat named Walter Kitty, a cuddly cat named Freddie Purrcury, and a very zippy dog named Lola.

YOU CAN DRAW FRANNY!

1. Draw two circles lightly with a pencil. (You will need to erase as you go along!)

2. Connect the circles for Franny's body and draw her nose.

3. Draw her arms, legs, and ears. Franny has short, wide ears!

4. Draw her eyes, her tail, and the lines for her overalls. Give Franny a smile!

5. Add all the details. Don't forget her whiskers!

6. Color in your drawing!

WHAT'S YOUR STORY?

Fritz and Franny love going to the amusement park.
Imagine **you** are going there with Fritz and Franny.
Which ride would you go on, and why?
Would Fritz and Franny go on it with you?
Write and draw your story!